LIQUID DESIRES

Also by Edward Sklepowich

Farewell to the Flesh

Death in a Serene City

LIQUID
DESIRES

An Urbino Macintyre Mystery

Edward Sklepowich

WILLIAM MORROW AND COMPANY, INC.
NEW YORK

It is the policy of William Morrow and Company, Inc., and its imprints and affiliates, recognizing the importance of preserving what has been written, to print the books we publish on acid-free paper, and we exert our best efforts to that end.

Library of Congress Cataloging-in-Publication Data

Sklepowich, Edward.
    Liquid desires : an Urbino Macintyre mystery / by Edward Sklepowich.
      p. cm.
    ISBN 0-688-11165-3
    I. Title.
PS3569.K574L56   1993
813'.54—dc20   92-21981
                                           CIP

Printed in the United States of America

First Edition

1 2 3 4 5 6 7 8 9 10

To my aunt and madrina
Anna Cacchillo Cusano

The one-line statements in Liquid Desires *are the "Truisms" of language artist Jenny Holzer, whose* Venice Installation *was the official United States exhibit at* La Biennale/XLIV esposizione internazionale d'arte, *1990.*

. . . to lose myself in the luminous and Venetian corpuscles of my Gala's glorious body.
—Salvador Dalí

PROLOGUE

Venice Melting

FORGET ABOUT VENICE sinking into the sea. Its fate this late July seemed to be to melt into the lagoon.

When Urbino Macintyre boarded the vaporetto two days ago to escape to the Lido, he had felt as if he were abandoning some vast diorama by Salvador Dalí.

Call it *The Persistence of Summer*, with the fabled stones of the city unstable and liquid, its winged lions reflected in golden pools of their own melting, the tower of the Moor clock dissolving into blues and bronzes, and the snowy domes of the Church of the Salute diminishing down into the Grand Canal like mammoth scoops of vanilla ice cream.

Even here on the veranda of the Grand Hotel des Bains with the Adriatic only two hundred feet away and a Campari soda within much easier reach, Urbino felt stifled this afternoon. If New Orleans had ever been this bad, memory mercifully failed him. Thoughts of New Orleans bringing, however, an unwelcome reminder of the imminent visit of his former brother-in-law, Eugene Hennepin, Urbino occupied his mind by reviewing the little drama he had been innocently caught up in yesterday afternoon at the Biennale modern art exhibit in the Giardini Pubblici, the Public Gardens.

It was his second visit to this year's exposition. He had been approaching the Italy Pavilion to take another look at the paintings by a group of Italian artists when a figure had stormed down the steps of the building and rushed past him. He could see that it was a woman, but caught only the briefest glimpse of a frightened, pale face behind large dark glasses. A plain brown scarf covered the woman's hair and she grasped a knife close to her side. Urbino moved instinctively away from the woman, as did the other people around him, as she went through the exit and became lost in the crowd. Several men ran after her from the Italy Pavilion, one of them a guard with his eyes streaming with tears.

When Urbino went into the building a few minutes later, he learned what had happened. The woman had slashed a controversial painting, *Nude in a Funeral Gondola,* by the Venetian artist Bruno Novembrini.

Against a background of a flooded Piazza San Marco, a beautiful nude woman with luminous, pearl-colored skin, bright green eyes, and a body less voluptuous than nubile was reclining seductively in a funeral gondola. She wore only emerald earrings, a thin gold bracelet, and a rose-colored Oriental turban that lent a glow to her face, longish neck, and breasts. She stared directly and provocatively at the viewer, one slim-fingered hand nestled between her legs like Titian's Naked Venus. The gondola, a deep shade of ebony, was draped in thick black material and overflowing with flowers and wreaths. At its prow was the Angel of Death with a torch. Another angel, this one bearded like a biblical patriarch, and a lion weeping into a black handkerchief hovered over the woman.

The attendants at the Italy Pavilion told Urbino that the vandal, whom no one recognized, had gone directly to the painting, slashed it in one swift motion, and then escaped after spraying a chemical substance at the two guards who tried to seize her.

Urbino now opened today's *Il Gazzettino*, where he found an account of the attack. The woman had not been apprehended. Massimo Zuin, the artist's Venetian dealer, said that the damage to the painting had not yet been assessed.

Urbino's good friend the Contessa da Capo-Zendrini, summering in her villa up in Asolo, would be amused to hear about the attack. She was sure to say that it was only what all this modern art deserved, and especially this particular painting, a reproduction of which she had seen in *Corriere della Sera*. The Contessa's comments on the Biennale were themselves as sharp as any knife brandished by a vandal could ever be. They hadn't become blunted since Urbino had first heard them at a Biennale reception ten years ago when he first met her.

During the previous Biennale, however, the modern art show had taken its revenge against her. It happened at the United States Pavilion at the exhibit of Jenny Holzer, an American artist who uses words as her medium and who won that year's coveted Golden Lion Award. The Contessa almost collapsed, so disagreeably affected had she been by the moving electronic lines of Holzer's text flashing ideological messages, pop psychology, and "mock clichés," as the artist herself called them, in five languages on the walls of a mausoleum-like room. One after another they had assaulted the Contessa:

A MAN CAN'T KNOW WHAT IT'S LIKE TO BE A WOMAN
ABUSE OF POWER COMES AS NO SURPRISE
EXPIRING FOR LOVE IS BEAUTIFUL BUT STUPID
AN ELITE IS INEVITABLE
HIDING YOUR MOTIVES IS DESPICABLE
KILLING IS UNAVOIDABLE BUT IS NOTHING TO BE
  PROUD OF
ROMANTIC LOVE WAS INVENTED TO MANIPULATE
  WOMEN
FATHERS OFTEN USE TOO MUCH FORCE
MOTHERS SHOULDN'T MAKE TOO MANY SACRIFICES
PRIVATE PROPERTY CREATED CRIME
ALL THINGS ARE DELICATELY INTERCONNECTED
MURDER HAS ITS SEXUAL SIDE
CHILDREN ARE THE MOST CRUEL OF ALL
I WILL KILL YOU FOR WHAT YOU MIGHT DO
DEATH CAME AND HE LOOKED LIKE A RAT WITH CLAWS
EVEN YOUR FAMILY CAN BETRAY YOU
MEN AREN'T MONOGAMOUS BY NATURE

Similar phrases had also been carved on the stone benches and in the marble floor tiles of the other rooms of the exhibit and had been printed on T-shirts, hats, posters, and billboards. They had been inescapable, even on the Venice water buses and in taxis across the lagoon in Mestre, but it was their electronic version at the United States Pavilion that had done the Contessa in.

She had reached for Urbino's shoulder and had him guide her to fresh air and sunlight, and then to a soothing *coppa* of gelato at the Caffè Paradiso outside the Biennale gates.

"I felt like that poor woman who went mad in the Marabar Caves in Forster's novel," she had said as she proceeded to spoon in her pistachio gelato. "My temples are still throbbing."

This year the Contessa was risking nothing. She was remaining cool and unruffled in her self-contained Villa La Muta in the hill town of Asolo not far from Venice. She vowed not to go anywhere near the Biennale grounds until every last piece of dubious art was crated back to where it should have stayed.

Continuing to page through the newspaper, Urbino came across a follow-up on a case that had shocked the city last week. A fifteen-year-old girl named Nicolina Ricci had been raped and murdered on one of the hottest days of the summer. Her parents, returning from an outing to the eastern shore of Lago di Garda, had found her naked body in her bedroom. The public had been spared none of the grisly details, including bloodstained bedsheets, multiple knife wounds, and the clump of hair gripped in one of Nicolina's hands. Today's paper reported that a forty-four-year-old man and close friend of the family, who lived alone in the same building, had confessed to the murder. Sexual obsession and the sultry sirocco, he said, had driven him mad.

Venice was a relatively quiet town, violence usually erupting on the mainland, but this summer had already seen Nicolina Ricci's vicious murder, the slashing of the painting at the modern art show, and several muggings of tourists in the less frequented alleys.

Urbino closed the paper. He looked off at the Adriatic, where the gray forms of ships were like ghosts on the horizon. A small plane droned over the water, and Vespas and bicycles passed along the Lungomare Marconi beyond the hedges of the hotel. A couple in a bicycle shay pedaled by, shaded beneath the floral canopy, and waved to him. An old man in a flat cap was crying *"Fragole fresche!"* outside the gates of the hotel. Urbino slipped off the veranda to buy a small box of the fresh strawberries and sat eating them as he mulled over what to do next.

Perhaps he would go down to the private strip of beach, take a swim, and then rest in one of the cabanas—just as he hoped to do tomorrow and the day after.

Urbino felt more than a little hedonistic in his *dolce far niente* existence at the Grand Hotel des Bains. Yet, although he might be "doing sweet nothing" here on the Lido, things hadn't been any better back at the Palazzo Uccello, where he had been trying to decide on his next biographical project and steeling himself for his ex–brother-in-law Eugene's visit.

Urbino was about to get up and go to his room to change his clothes for the beach when a welcome, familiar voice greeting one of the staff floated up to him from the brick pavement below the veranda. It was the Contessa da Capo-Zendrini. As she came slowly up the shell-shaped stone stairs, Urbino went over to her.

"Barbara, whatever are you doing here?"

The Contessa turned with a smile of mild exasperation on her attractive face. She wore a blue-and-green Fortuny dress that had once belonged to her mother and a pert straw hat. A furled green parasol was under her arm.

"To rescue you from all these purple hydrangeas and fronds and take you back to Asolo with me—and not just for my garden party tomorrow but for the rest of the summer. Don't tell me that you haven't the time! Look at the way you're languishing here like Aschenbach in your cream-colored suit! I know how you can allow yourself to sink indecently into summer. I insist that you do it up in Asolo."

Urbino kissed her cheek. It was pleasantly cool.

"Milo's waiting with the boat. You can go right home to pack and to get Serena, if you like." Serena was the cat Urbino had rescued on a wet November day in the Giardini Pubblici where the Biennale was held. "The car's at the Piazzale Roma."

"I can only come for the weekend, Barbara."

"Don't tell me you prefer a hotel to La Muta."

The Contessa looked around the veranda, where guests were absorbed in nothing more strenuous than their own sedentary pleasures. She wrinkled her nose, as if the Grand Hotel were a mere pensione with smelly drains and an obligatory breakfast of burned coffee and damp crackers.

"Have you forgotten that my ex–brother-in-law Eugene is coming up from Florence on Monday?"

"Can't you think of a less unwieldy way of referring to the poor man?" she reprimanded him as she sat down. "It's been ages since you were married to his sister."

"But that's the way I think of him."

"I'm afraid it means you haven't yet let go, *caro*, but I've never been one for psychologizing." She put her parasol on an empty wicker chair. "I'll have a *Coppa Fornarina*," she said, naming her favorite macaroon-and-cherry-garnished gelato she always ordered at Florian's. "They do have them here, don't they?"

"I'm sure they can make one, Barbara."

After ordering the Contessa's ice cream concoction and another Campari soda for himself—this time bolstered with some white wine—Urbino asked her how things were in Asolo.

"If you came more often than once or twice a month you wouldn't have to ask! Bands of teenagers have been running around pulling up plants and breaking windows. It makes me almost happy not to have had any children. They'd be going through the difficult years now."

Urbino let the Contessa's exaggeration pass. If she and Alvise had had children, even the youngest would have long passed through its difficult years. The Contessa must be approaching sixty, but suspicion was the closest he would come to truth until her seventy-fifth birthday when she promised a revelation. Urbino, twenty years her junior, felt that she was entitled to her vanity, especially since she looked a good ten years younger than sixty.

"I hope you appreciate my taking time out from all the preparations for the garden party to coax you into the hills of Asolo, *caro*. By the way, I broke down and extended a neighborly invitation to that retired American actress you've been wanting to meet—the one who's always parading around in pants and a turban and probably just waiting to break out in a leopard print and boa! *I've* never heard of her," the Contessa said a little too lightly, "but Silvestro has told me all about her."

Silvestro Occhipinti was the eighty-year-old longtime friend of the Contessa's dead husband, Alvise. In need of money, he rented out his villa to foreigners—currently the retired actress Madge Lennox—while living in several rooms in the center of Asolo.

"This impertinent person in pants is my last attempt to try

to persuade you gently to grace us all with your presence. I know you don't like *les grandes fêtes,* my dear, but this is my very own. If you refuse again, I'm prepared to have Milo strong-arm you."

The waiter brought the gelato and the Campari soda. For a few minutes the Contessa enjoyed her *coppa* in self-indulgent silence before filling him in on the gossip in Asolo. The most interesting was the story of a young American man who had been trying to gain devious access to Freya Stark, the well-known British traveler and writer, who had made Asolo her home for decades. The Contessa somehow held Urbino, as both a biographer and an American, responsible for the intrusion of his countryman.

The Contessa turned silent again and ate the rest of her *coppa* with the restrained enthusiasm of a well-bred child.

"You look as if you could use a pick-me-up yourself," she said when she finished. "Why don't we order you some gelato? Alcohol is going to debilitate you in this heat."

"Would you like another *coppa* yourself, Barbara?"

"Most definitely not."

But despite the Contessa's refusal Urbino knew she was tempted, the only thing holding her back being not satiation or the fear of gaining weight—something she seemed to be bless-edly immune to—but the embarrassment of being seen to in-dulge in two *coppe* in a row. She would be more than willing, however, to have her seconds somewhere else.

"An even better remedy than gelato for your haggard look, *caro,* would be La Muta," the Contessa persisted. "The fresh air will do wonders for you! I'll take better care of you than they do here—and it won't cost you a single, solitary lira. You *are* coming back with me, aren't you?" There was a plaintive look on her face. "It's just that I miss you so abominably. Doesn't my coming here all the way from Asolo on one of the hottest days of the summer prove that?"

"I've missed you, too, Barbara. Of course I'll come."

"Do you think I'll get to meet this ex–brother-in-law of yours, or are you going to keep him a big, dark secret like so many other things in your past?"

"You'll meet him. You might even like him better than me."

"An impossibility of the most impossible kind, *caro*—even if your Eugene is handsomer and younger than you are. I'm yours forever, a fate I haven't chosen. But I do hope he has some tales—or would he call them 'yarns'?—to tell of the days when your hair was as bright as Huckleberry Finn's and you hadn't yet become jaded!" She reached for her parasol. "Finish your drink and let's make a gracious but quick exit. I'll be walking in the garden while you arrange things. We might even have time for a real *Coppa Fornarina* at Florian's before we leave. This one"—she nodded down at the empty goblet—"left a lot to be desired."

Making no comment, Urbino signaled for the waiter.